HELLO KITTY®
and
♥ME♥

Happy Birthday

Published by Sourcebooks Jabberwocky, an imprint of Sourcebooks, Inc.
P.O. Box 4410, Naperville, Illinois 60567-4410
(630) 961-3900
Fax: (630) 961-2168
www.jabberwockykids.com

Library of Congress Cataloging-in-Publication data is on file with the publisher.

Source of Production: Worzalla, Stevens Point WI, USA
Date of Production: August 2014
Run Number: 5002116

Printed and bound in the United States of America.
WOZ 10 9 8 7 6 5 4 3 2 1

HELLO KITTY® and ♥ME♥

Happy Birthday

Hello Kitty and her twin sister, Mimmy, are excited. Today is their birthday!

It's a perfect day for a birthday picnic.
All of their friends are coming!

Hello Kitty and Mimmy are helping Mama make cupcakes. They want to make sure you have a cupcake, too.

What kind of cupcakes do you like?

Fifi and Thomas are bringing balloons.

Tracy is bringing party hats.
What colors are the hats?

Dear Daniel and Jodie are bringing cookies.

Can you find Joey?
He's dressed for the party!

Tim and Tammy
are bringing a birthday card.
How many balloons are on the card?

Hello, friends!
Let's play hide-and-seek before the picnic!

Can you find all the friends?
Look for the party hats!

Here we are!
Now it's time for the picnic!

Mmm, yummy cupcakes!
Small and sweet, they are fun to eat!

Yummy cookies, too!
Soft and chewy, warm and gooey!

Oh no!
What does Hello Kitty see?

What do you think might happen next?

It's a rainstorm! Hello Kitty and Mimmy's perfect party will be ruined!

Hello Kitty has an idea.
What do you think she is going to do?

Umbrellas!
Good thinking, Hello Kitty!

Rain or shine, good friends
make every party perfect.

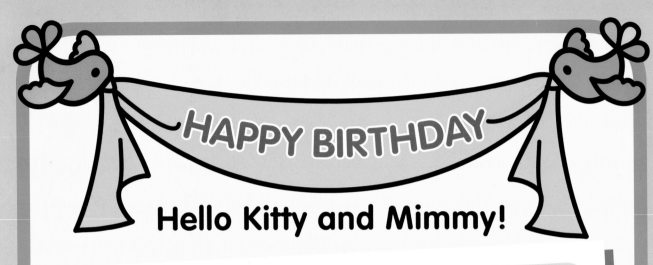

HAPPY BIRTHDAY

Hello Kitty and Mimmy!